THE APPLE WAR

THE APPLE WAR

Written and illustrated by Bernice Myers

Parents' Magazine Press / New York

The Apple War first appeared in The Way of the World
from the Holt Basic Reader Series, edited by Drs.
Weiss and Everetts, published 1973 by Holt, Rinehart
& Winston. Used with permission.

Library of Congress Cataloging in Publication Data

Myers, Bernice.
  The apple war.

  SUMMARY: Should the war be held before or after the
kings's birthday party? That is the question.
  [1. War—Fiction] I. Title.
PZ7.M9817Ap   [E]   72-8191
ISBN 0-8193-0650-9   ISBN 0-8193-0651-7 (lib. bdg.)

For Marc

..."They're my apples,"
said King Sam.

"It's my tree,"
said King Oscar.

"But,"
said King Sam,
"the branches
hang over on
my land."

"The apples are
on the branches of
MY tree
and
MY tree
stands on
MY land!"
shouted King Oscar.

"The apples
may be on YOUR tree
but they
fall
on MY land,"
said King Sam.
"So,
the apples are mine."

"They're not!"
said King Oscar.

"They are!"
shouted King Sam.

"ARE! Are! Are!"
said King Sam.
"This means war!
And I mean
WAR!"

"I'm ready anytime,"
said King Oscar.

"How's June 5th!"
asked King Sam.
"It falls on a Monday."

"Suits me just fine.
I'll see you then!"

Time passed, and
on the morning of
June 4th,
King Sam
called for
William.
"Find out
if King Oscar
is ready for our war
tomorrow."

"But King,
you can't have a war
tomorrow.
It's your birthday!"
said William.

"You're right!
I forgot!"
the king said.
"But I can't
call off a war
at the last minute.
It wouldn't be polite.
Besides,
a promise is a promise."

"What about the
party
you always have?
I've already invited
everyone to
come,"
puffed William.

King Sam was upset.
He wanted to keep
his promise.
But he didn't know
what
to do.
"I know!" he said,
"I'll hide."

"A king doesn't hide,"
said William.

"Then say I'm sick . . .
Or I broke my leg . . .
Or my mother won't let me . . ."

But
William
wasn't listening.
He was thinking.

"I have it!"
William suddenly shouted.
"Fight the war
first, and
then have the party,
or have the party
and then the war!"

"Wonderful, wonderful!"
said King Sam.
"I'll have the party
and then the war.
No! No!
The war
and then the party.
Party…war…
war…party—
Oh, I can't make up my mind
now.

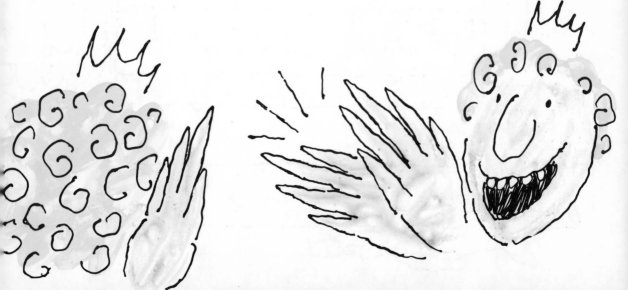

"I'm going to sleep.
I can think better
in the morning."

The next day when
King Sam awoke
he began
at once
to think.
He walked back and forth
and around and around.
Sometimes
he waved his arms
in the air.
At last
he made up
his mind.
"I'll fight the war
first
and have the
rest of the day
for my
party."

He put on his
armor
jumped on his
horse
and rode off toward
the battlefield.

His army was there
waiting for
his command.

"CHARGE!" he shouted.

"HEY!
WAIT!
STOP!
HOLD IT!
IT'S ME!"
called William,
riding up to
the king.

"If you have the war
first
there might not be
anyone left
to come to
your party."

"You're right.
I never thought
of that,"
said King Sam.
"So we'll
have the party
first
and then
the war."

King Oscar was
signaling
from the other side
of the battlefield.

And
King Sam waved back.
"We'll fight
this afternoon, Oscar.
First
we're going to have
my party."

And right there
in the middle of the
battlefield
the tables were set
and everyone
began to eat . . .
and sing . . .

and eat . . .
and talk . . .
and
eat and eat and . . .

They were having such a
good time
that no one wanted to
fight
anymore.

"You still mad?"
asked King Sam.

"No. You mad?"
asked King Oscar.

"Me? Mad?
Why should I be mad?"
asked King Sam.

"Then what were we
going to
fight about?"
asked King Oscar.

"I can't remember,"
said King Sam.

With that
the two kings
looked at each other
and began to
laugh.
So did the armies.

"Pay us
a visit
sometime,"
said King Sam.
"I'm having a cookout
tomorrow.
Why don't you bring the
wife and kids?"

"Maybe I will,"
said King Oscar.
"Say,
I like the way
your armor
shines.
What polish do you use?"

"I'll send you
a bottle," said King Sam.

"Thanks," said King Oscar.

"Here . . .

have one of my apples."

"YOUR apples!". . .

BERNICE MYERS was born in New York and has lived in the northeast United States all her life, except for four years in Paris early in her marriage. Turned on to writing for children by a lecture delivered by Jan Balet, she found her first efforts rejected, but was accepted as an illustrator. She has subsequently written and illustrated a good number of books, the most recent being *Chicken Feathers*, *My Mother Is Lost*, and *Sh h h h! It's a Secret*. *The Apple War* is her first book for Parents' Magazine Press. Mrs. Myers, her husband, and two sons live in Peekskill, New York.